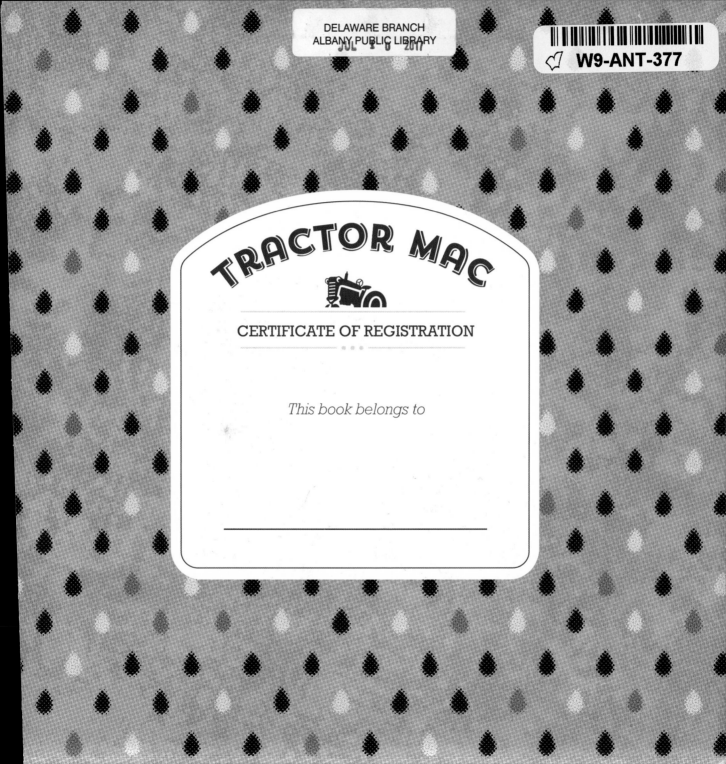

TRACTOR MAC

CERTIFICATE OF REGISTRATION

This book belongs to

_____

ALSO BY BILLY STEERS

TRACTOR MAC
WORTH THE WAIT

Written and illustrated by
BILLY STEERS

FARRAR STRAUS GIROUX · NEW YORK

FARMER BILL was looking over the garden at Stony Meadow Farm.

"The watermelons are coming along great this year. We may have one good enough to enter in the Fruit and Vegetable Show."

"With time, these will become big, sweet melons," thought Tractor Mac.

"They take so long to grow," said Pete the pig to his brother, Paul.

The next day the two pigs checked for signs of growth.

"Maybe we could make them get bigger faster," said Paul.

"Great idea!" said Pete. "I saw Tractor Mac use his cultivator like this."

He rooted around the young plants.

"I'll give the dirt a drink," said Paul.

"We can prune the vines and fertilize
the soil like Farmer Bill does," said Pete.
"I didn't know farming was so easy!"
squealed Paul.

"We can sort the melons by size," said Paul.

"Good thinking," said Pete.

"We should stack the melons so they'll be easy to harvest when they're ready," said Pete.

"Pete and Paul, watermelon experts!" cheered Paul.

When Farmer Bill finally saw what was left of his melons, he was not very happy.

"It looks like a hurricane came through here," thought Tractor Mac.

"Silly pigs," said Farmer Bill with a sigh. "That's the end of my melon patch for this year. Now we won't have any melons to enter in the Fruit and Vegetable Show, let alone many to eat."

"We just wanted the watermelons
to grow faster," grunted Pete.

"I guess we're not very good farmers,"
groaned Paul.

"Plants take time to grow," said Tractor Mac.

"You can't rush them," added Sibley the horse.

"Cheer up, boys!" clucked Carla the chicken. "I've found something you should see over here."

"It's a baby melon!" gasped Pete.

"How could we have missed that right here in our own pen?" asked Paul.

"It must have grown from seeds in the melons given to you in your feed trough," said Tractor Mac. "You could raise this one to full size."

"But we might wreck it," said Pete.

"We don't have very good luck with melons," said Paul.

"Why don't you give it a try and see what happens?" asked Tractor Mac.

Pete gently cleaned around the small vine. Paul carefully gave it a little water.

"It's not growing," said Paul.

"Be patient and don't hurry it," said Tractor Mac.

Day after day, the animals on the farm watched
as the pigs cared for their melon. The melon slowly
grew. Pete shooed away bugs and caterpillars.

"Foo!" huffed Pete.

Paul chased away other pests that might have wanted a tasty bite.

"Scat!" oinked Paul. It turned out that the pigpen was a good spot for growing watermelons, and their melon got bigger over time.

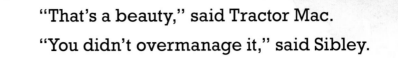

"That's a beauty," said Tractor Mac.

"You didn't overmanage it," said Sibley.

"You cared for it just right," mooed Margot the cow.

"It was worth the wait," said Pete with a smile.

The next morning Pete and Paul awoke to check on their melon.

"It's gone!" wailed Pete. "Someone stole our watermelon!"

"Who could do this?" sobbed Paul. "We were so careful and patient!"

"It'll be okay," said Tractor Mac as he wheeled over to the sty.

"We'll find out in due time what happened."

A day later, Farmer Bill brought home a surprise.

"I found this watermelon in your pen and had to enter it in the Fruit and Vegetable Show," he said. "It won People's Choice! We'll save the seeds and grow more winning melons next year, with the help of my special pig farmers, of course!"

The few watermelons that had survived the patch disaster and ripened were shared with all the animals on the farm.

"Maybe we could try beans and squash next!" said Paul.

"Or pumpkins and tomatoes!" said Pete.

"Just be patient," said Tractor Mac with a wink. "Next year will be here soon enough."

To Pete and Paul, my other brothers

Farrar Straus Giroux Books for Young Readers
An imprint of Macmillan Publishing Group, LLC
175 Fifth Avenue, New York 10010

Color separations by Bright Arts (H.K.) Ltd.
Printed in China by Toppan Leefung Printing Ltd.,
Dongguan City, Guangdong Province
Designed by Kristie Radwilowicz
First edition, 2017
1   3   5   7   9   10   8   6   4   2

mackids.com

Library of Congress Cataloging-in-Publication Data
Title: Tractor Mac worth the wait / written and illustrated by Billy Steers.
Description: New York: Farrar Straus Giroux (BYR), 2017. | Series: Tractor Mac | Summary:
    "The pigs, Pete and Paul, learn the importance of patience when they try (unsuccessfully) to
    speed along the growth of Farmer Bill's prized watermelons"—Provided by publisher.
Identifiers: LCCN 2016034915 | ISBN 9780374301156 (hardback)
Subjects: | CYAC: Tractors—Fiction. | Pigs—Fiction. | Patience—Fiction. | Farm life—Fiction.
    | BISAC: JUVENILE FICTION / Transportation / General. | JUVENILE FICTION /
    Lifestyles / Farm & Ranch Life.
Classification: LCC PZ7.S81536 Tw 2017 | DDC [E]—dc23
LC record available at https://lccn.loc.gov/2016034915

Our books may be purchased in bulk for promotional, educational, or business use.
Please contact your local bookseller or the Macmillan Corporate and Premium Sales Department
at (800) 221-7945 ext. 5442 or by e-mail at MacmillanSpecialMarkets@macmillan.com.

ABOUT THE AUTHOR

Billy Steers is an author, illustrator, and commercial pilot. In addition to the Tractor Mac series, he has worked on forty other children's books. Mr. Steers had horses and sheep on the farm where he grew up in Connecticut. Married with three sons, he still lives in Connecticut. Learn more about the Tractor Mac books at www.tractormac.com.